Ordinary

Publication Date: 24th July 2020

Hariram Suthakaran: Author

This story is based on true events.

ISBN: 9798668934492

To My Loving Sister
and my best friend
Aaron.

Part 1 | Aaron

ORDINARY

My name is Aaron. I know I am normal, but I don't know. I mean yeah, I feel normal inside but on the outside, no. I have autism. This makes me a hard learner; like I don't catch on to things quickly and I can read and write but slowly.

I can play every game
you can tell me except
Tag, ball, hide and
seek since the pressure
on those games makes
me faint.

Due to this, I don't
have many friends,
but James and Lowell
always stick by my
side.

They already go to school, and I am home-schooled since children always laugh and try to play pranks on me.

These two kids, Isla and Kasia, pranked me for a whole day when I came and visited the school to see if I fit in.

My mum and dad
have always been
afraid of my safety
and hence why they
have never sent me to
school since the
incident that
happened.

My brother Harry is
not just brother to me;

he is my best friend, and I would never trade anyone for him. He is like my knight in shining armour, that will always protect me.

The only truth I know about me is that no matter what people say, I am a normal boy.

STARTING

SCHOOL

I'm starting school again in two days, and I am not ready. My parents never asked for my consent. I am so scared, and I don't think I'm going to fit in. The even more angry part is that my parents won't also send me to the same school as James and Lowell. I mean that is uncalled for.

I'm ten, so I think I'm going into grade 4.

Home-schooling has been a part of my life for more than

seven years, minus one day.

My parents are trying to figure out a way for me to try and make me relax because I can have anxiety attacks quite quickly and so they are worried that I

may need so
support.

I have seen these
movies were a
disabled boy goes to
school and gets
made fun of, so this
just makes twice the
amount of scared
and not only that
Harry started saying

that school is
difficult which made
triple the amount of
frightened I was.

MY

SUPPORT

ANIMAL

My parents came up
to me with a present. I
opened up the gift, and
it had a dog.

It took me a while to
process, but then I
realised it was my
support animal for
school.

“Surprise, honey. Your stuff for school and a dog that is now your support animal.” Said, Mrs Robin

I took everything and ran upstairs so I can give my dog some clothes.

I felt like the happiest
boy living and was
determined to make
my first day at school
exciting and fun.

FIRST DAY

ENTRANCE

I had a scared feeling, not going to lie, but I knew I had to get through it. I walked to school with dad and once we arrived and I left he started crying. My dog, who I named Thomas,

started barking, but
I made him quiet
because he began to
draw a crowd.

People were asking
questions to me like

"Why do have that
beast?"

Or

"I'm allergic, you know!"

I ignored them and went to the principal's office to talk to him about his classes and about the work they will give. I was worried that the work they will provide would be too hard for me and that I could not be able to complete the task.

HEADMASTER'S

OFFICE

I walked in with my handshaking. When I entered, I was greeted with a sweet smile. Mr Lynch, the principal, used to know my mum since they were classmates.

"Good Morning, Aaron. How are you?" asked Mr Lynch

"Godd, I mean good sir," I said mistakenly

"Well, what I have you came to discuss?" said Mrs Lynch

My dog started barking so I tied him to a leash so he would be quiet.

"Well, my classes. How hard is the work? What lessons am I taking? How big is the school? Where are the classes?"

Mr Lynch cleared everything up for me and gave my dog a

treat, and I got a map.

I left the room and as I was walking out, I ran into Elizabeth Jones. She was a disabled girl. She was paralysed from the leg to the foot so

she could not move
her leg or foot.

Elizabeth started
shouting at me and
my dog ran away
because I had
fainted.

THE MOMENT I

LEARNED

THE TRUTH

I did not know he had anxiety and autism. I just thought that he walked around with that dog for fun.

A boy named Oliver came up to the place he fainted, and he asked who made him faint.

I put my hand up knowing that I was

going to be shouted
at.

Oliver started to
explain to me that he
had a disability and
could not stand the
pressure.

The headmaster
came and ordered

everyone to go to
homeroom and me
and Oliver to stay.

FIRST AID

ROOM

Aaron awoke in the first aid room having no memory whatsoever of what happened.

Mr Lynch ordered as to be friends with him no matter what. He also told us that we could not leave

that room until
further notice.

We played all sorts
of games like rock,
paper scissors and
UNO. He started
talking to us really
fluently because last

he could not speak
very well. It was
then time for us all
to go to class and
Aaron was not
ready.

Part 3 | Oliver

FIRST

CLASS

"Kids, you can go to class. Just be

careful," said Mr Lynch

We started class late and never even went to homeroom. I felt bad for Aaron. He had to take the dog everywhere since it was his emotional support animal.

We went to our first class where our teacher, Mrs Rawlings, was taking her English class register.

"Is Aaron here?" asked the Teacher

"Umm Yes, Teacher," replied Aaron

"Call me Mrs Rawlings." said the Teacher

Aaron was stuck on the worksheet he was given so I

helped him. He felt really needy at that point and felt like he was going to have a panic attack, so I told him the answers to question 17-21.

He is a sweet boy, but he just needs to get the aspects of

how school works, so
I decided to have a
word with Mr
Lynch.

MR LYNCH

"Hello, Oliver. How can I help?" asked Mr Lynch

"Well, you know Aaron, he does not know where everything is located and really needs help with his work. If you don't mind can I be his personal tutor?"

Mr Lynch looked confused and I could tell that he was not fond of the idea, so I made the idea a little better."

"I will not only teach him maths and English but Science as well and I will teach him after school from 4 pm to 4:30 pm. I will start next week Friday."

This must have made him really excited about the idea because he agreed really quickly.

Part 4 | Aaron

TUTOR

I was called into Mr Lynch's office by Oliver. I was worried since I had already seen him 5 times in one day.

I arrived and as always, he had a happy face.

"James, sit down. I need a word." Said Mr Lynch

"What is it, sir? I asked

'Well, Oliver is going to be tutoring you for the term." Said Mr Lynch

I was scared if I had done that bad in class even though Oliver did help me and tell me answers through 17 to 21.

In the end, I agreed with Mr Lynch and decided to take daily tutor lessons with

Oliver from Friday next week.

MATHS CLASS

During maths we had a teach called Mrs Hawkes. She

had freckles all over her face.

She started taking register and then I realised that I had left my bag in Mr Lynch's office.

I did not know what to do so I asked James if I could borrow his pencil and of course he said yes.

I kind of always enjoyed maths. During home-schooling that was

the easiest subject,
so I was happy when
the work they gave
was similar to what
my home-school
teacher gave me.

LUNCH

BREAK

**My dog was outside
the whole time
playing with his little**

football. The teachers found his barking very "Annoying", but I bet they were just jealous that they can't bring dogs to school.

Elizbeth and Oliver came out and we

started playing
manhunt, a game
that combines two of
my least favourite
games, Hide and
Seek and Tag.

They taught me how
to stay calm and
focused during the
game and since I

was doing so well,
they taught me
basketball.

Me and my dog
Thomas played
football too, so I
would say that was a
successful lunch
break

LIBRARY

HOUR

Every week, we go to the library for what

our teacher calls
Library Time, a time
to express our little
reading hearts with
words. I find the
name hilarious, but I
don't mention It.

I love this time
because all kids
must stay quiet since

It was a library. This meant I could relax while reading a book. I started reading Harry Potter and The Half-Blood Prince by J.K Rowling and I loved It. I got so far Into the book that I even reserved It.

MUSIC

Our final class of the
day was music and
by far that was my
favourite lesson. We
practised drums In
today's lesson, and
It was really fun.

My dog, Thomas
was Inside the
classroom because

our teacher, Miss C was being really nice.

Elizabeth and Oliver also loved my pet dog and they looked after It as If It was theirs.

THE DRIVE

BACK

HOME

My mum and came and picked me up and she could tell I was happy with my first day. She was smiling like a baby when you tickle it. I knew she was proud of me but then she started asking me really annoying questions like how

my first day was and
if I made friends.

I somehow managed
to recap my whole
day in less than 5
minutes to my mum.

She was so proud
she decided to make
a cake for me.

TEA TIME

I went upstairs and got changed into my normal indoor clothes.

My mum was so happy she made tea time an hour early.

My brother, Harry,
was not so happy
about his first day.

He started to
complain about how
no one would listen
to him speak and
that no child should
be treated that way.

I ignored and just started eating my cake.

My dad had suddenly changed his mind on whether I should I go to school. I thought he was just joking but he called Mr Lynch

and was about to
pull me out of the
school, until my
mum hang up the
phone.

"Honey, why?"
Mum asked

"Look at harry. He turned into a mess when he started normal school."

"Aaron was just telling me in the car that he was having the best time at school and that he even made two friends."

"Alright, report cards go out next month, when the term holiday starts. If Aaron gets better grades then Harry, he won't be pulled out of school." Said my Dad

My mum sadly agreed, and I could not do anything to stop them agreeing to the deal.

REPORT CARD

I spent a month in Oliver's tuition class. I had improved like lighting in English and Science and I was ready for my report card.

They were posted to
our parents and my
one arrived a day
before Harry's, so
we had to wait.

Then when they
came, I was shocked.

My report card

English	98%
Maths	99%
Science	95%
History	89%
Music	87%

"Aaron is a
wonderful student.

No autistic kid has got this good grade. There is an award ceremony after the term ends and Aaron is invited."

My brother's report card

English	61%
Maths	54%
Science	7%
History	67%
Music	34%
French	2%

"Your son, Harry is a disruption to this school. I would love to expel him but at South High School we try and take pride in every student."

Then a random note came out of my brother's report card.

"Your son James is invited to join 10 other students this holiday at study camp. We will be practising the many things he got wrong such us, French, Science, Music etc.

Address: 99 High Street Camp, NYC, 437883

*Please make sure he arrives
promptly in his school
uniform ready to learn.”*

Signed,

Mrs Dix,

Leader of Education

My father screamed
his head off at my
brother, then he
congratulated me.
My mum was very
happy too. I texted
Oliver immediately.

TEXTING

TIME

To Oliver: My
best friend

From Aaron

Hey, Oliver.
Thanks to your
tutoring lessons, I
am not being

pulled out of school."

To Aaron: A nice dude

From Oliver

OMG! That is great news. I got all 100% except music. Ugh, I wish I could quit it.

To Oliver: My best friend

From Aaron

LOL! I wish I could quit music as well since that was the lowest grade on my whole report card.

Guess, we will see each other next week in November, bye.

To Aaron: A nice dude

From Oliver

I guess so. Bye.

Part 5 | Harry

ANNOYED

"You are grounded!" shouted dad

"But I thought I did so well." I said

"Turns out you did not."

I was surprised to see that I had failed every subject.

Aaron ran upstairs with a smirk on his face.

I could tell he was
happy that he was not
going to be pulled out
of school

Once Aaron had left
dad had cancelled all
my tutoring lessons
and called me a
"WASTE OF
MONEY"

Not only that now I need to go to this random study camp thing and so this really sucks.

Part 6 | Aaron

BACK AT

SCHOOL

Back to school was not perfect. Not perfect at all. Elizabeth hates me for some reason and Oliver is paying less

attention to me when
I'm speaking to him.

I was walking in when
I realized I forget my
dog. I called my mom
she had sad news.

"Thomas is…"

"WHAT?" I shouted

"Dead. He is really sick, and he is at the vet and we think is dead."

"But….no. It can't be."

"I will call you back,
Aaron."

I felt a hint of
depression. I ran to
Mr Lynch's office.

"Hello Aaron. Are you
her because of your
dog?"

"Yes, what should I do?"

"Just try and forget about it>"

I left his office and an 8th Grade pushed me because I did not move out of the way.

His name was Emil.
He punched me and
pushed me, and my
teeth fell out.

Part 7 | Emil

MY BAD

I pushed him out of
the way on purpose.
if you mess with me,
YOU GET MY
FISTS.

I was called into the principal's office.

"Emil, I find your behaviour unacceptable. A boy is bleeding his head out and is in hospital. Not only that this could affect his health."

"What do you mean
affect his health."

"He has autism."

I never knew he had
autism. My brother
has autism so I
should now how it

feels. I did not respond after the headteacher.

"Your parents are coming and your suspended for 2 weeks."

My parents was shouting at me like crazy. They made me apologize by email since I was suspended.

To:

aaron54@gmail.
com

From:

emildabeast@
gmail.com

Sorry dude. I
get stressed
really quick and
you not moving
just made me
angry.

To: Mr Lynch

From Emil

I am sorry for
punching Aaron.
I will never do

again, I was
just under
pressure

To: Emil

From Mr Lynch

Thank you for
your apology.
Aaron is in
hospital and
could be
paralyzed.
Sadly, I am

going to have
to expel you.

To:emildabeast
@gmail.com

From:aaron54@
gmail.com

No problem. I
am going to be
in hospital for
a while, but I
think I can get
better, I just

have head
damage.

Part 8 | Aaron

MESSAGE

WITH

OLIVER

From:
oliverking@gmail.com

To:
aaron54@gmail.com

Hey dude.
Heard about
your accident.
Sorry, I was not
there to help.
sorry!!! please
forgive me!!

To:

oliverking@gmail.com

From:

aaron54@gmail.com

It's fine. We
are best friends
still. My dog is
at the vet and
he could die.

From:

oliverking@gmail.

com

To:

aaron54@gmail.c

om

Oh, that is so sad. Hope he gets well soon. See you next time at school.

To
oliverking@gmail.
com From:
aaron54@gmail.c
om

See you at

school.

HALLOWEEN

I was left out of the hospital on 31th October at 15:00 just in time Halloween. I was so happy because I am never allowed except on my

birthday, Halloween
or Christmas.

My parents started
becoming way more
careful about me.
They even banned me
from the park.

When it was Halloween,
I went as a clown. My
brother was going to be
a skeleton, but he was
grounded for low grades.

Oliver came to my house
to do trick-o-treating
with me.

There was a house in front of me and they let us take us much candy as possible.

When I came home, I officially declared Halloween as SUCCESFUL, but my head hurt really badly due to my accident

EVERYONE HATES ME

Everyone hated me at school, since I "snitched" on him even though the

principal came when the incident happen.

During lunch I went to where Oliver was sitting. He was sitting with a girl called Sunshine.

"Hi, I am Sunshine."

"Hello!" I said

"Hey, Aaron. How's
your dog?" asked Oliver

"Haven't heard from the
vet." I said

For lunch, I had string
cheese, ham sandwich
and a pudding cup.

School was very different no one would like me, and they would not take pity or anything else.

Classes were shorter and I would normally be taken out 30 minutes before every class for a special interview.

CHRISTMAS

HOLIDAY

Two months went by and I had kind of gotten used to the annoying, new schedule of mine. It was 22nd December and the last day of term. I had started growing

feelings for Sunshine
since I sat with her every
day, non-stop during
lunch; now she is even in
my class.

She had the most
amazing face and her
teeth would shine like
the sun on the heatwave.

Anyways I have never
had a fun Christmas

because my aunt Susan comes. She is always so mean, but this time she is not coming because she has a cold. This made me really happy though.

BACK FROM WINTER BREAK

Mr Lynch was greeting all the kids who came back from summer break. Sadly, I had to get glasses, which made me look like a nerd. Not only that, Mr Lynch put me in the CSNHC (Children of Special Needs Honours Class).

They always put the honour students on a wall so when I the whole school found out that I had Autism.

I got more respect somehow and was actually treated like a normal school boy. This to me seemed like

the perfect back to
school.

I ASKED HER

I was really scared but
I go the courage to ask
out, Sunshine.

I gave her a card and
flowers, and she came

up to me and gave me
a kiss on the cheek and
left. I knew this meant
yes and so I was super
happy.

Summer

The heat was unbearable. Oliver and I played tag, but it just ended up with me fainting for 10 seconds.

My dig also died. He
had eaten a nail which
poked his tummy
leading to his death

I have gotten used to
my autism and school
My headmaster, my
friends they are all my
family no matter how
much they either
annoy or hurt, that

school will be in. my hearts for the years to come.

We took our final summer exams and those moving to 6th grade had to make a promise. It was:

"I will not be unkind to teachers, staff or any other faculty member. I will treat all kids with respect. I declare that I am going to be the top of the school at 6th Grade"

My report card for the end of school was also AMAZING!

Maths	100%
English	99%
Science	97%
History	97%
Music	94%
N/A	N/A

I entered this school
year thinking that I

would be a freak, with
a dog but I finished
with a bang and
remember:

"Never judge an
autistic by their
outside appearance."

Part 9 | Narrator

Aaron had a sense of pride for the whole school year. He had taken many speech therapy and physical therapy to improve his English and fitness.

Sunshine and Aaron had made it official.

Oliver had become the besties with Aaron and Elizabeth.

Elizbeth apologized to him for being a really rude person by ignoring him.

**This story is based on
a true story**